Scholastic Children's Books
An imprint of Scholastic Ltd
Euston House, 24 Eversholt Street, London, NW1 1DB, UK
Registered office: Westfield Road, Southam, Warwickshire, CV47 0RA
SCHOLASTIC and associated logos are trademarks and/or
registered trademarks of Scholastic Inc.

First published in the US by Random House Children's Books, a division of Penguin
Random House LLC, 2017
First published in the UK by Scholastic Ltd, 2017

ISBN 978 1407 17138 8

A CIP catalogue record for this book
is available from the British Library.

Printed by CPI Group (UK) Ltd, Croydon, CR0 4YY
Papers used by Scholastic Children's Books are made
from wood grown in sustainable forests.

1 3 5 7 9 10 8 6 4 2

This is a work of fiction. Names, characters, places, incidents
and dialogues are products of the author's imagination or are used
fictitiously. Any resemblance to actual people, living or dead,
events or locales is entirely coincidental.

www.scholastic.co.uk

DREAMWORKS

Trolls

POPPY AND THE MANE MANIA!

BY DAVE LEWMAN

SCHOLASTIC

CHAPTER 1

Early one bright sunny morning, Poppy ran through Troll Village towards the Hair in the Air Salon. She didn't want to be late for her appointment with Maddy, the Trolls' expert hair stylist. Poppy's poof of pink hair had to be absolutely perfect for the big party that night!

As she ran, Poppy sang a happy, bouncy song about getting her hair done. *"This Troll feels like she's floating on air ... after Maddy styles her hair! Uh huh! Yeah, yeah! C'mon! Get it, get it!"*

She'd purposefully scheduled her appointment

with Maddy for first thing in the morning so she'd be the only customer in the salon. Poppy loved the peace and quiet of the empty hair salon. She'd close her eyes and listen to the snip snip snip of Maddy's scissors. Smell the shampoo and hairspray. Feel the comb running through her hair...

But it didn't turn out that way.

When Poppy opened the door of the Hair in the Air Salon, the colourful pod was already bustling with customers! Maddy was running from station to station, working on several Trolls' hair at the same time. She went from washing to drying to brushing to trimming without missing a beat.

"Good morning, Poppy!" the Trolls all shouted happily.

"Here to get your hair done for the big party?" Cooper asked as Maddy worked on his blue dreadlocks.

"You know it!" Poppy said enthusiastically. She giggled. "Looks like I'm not the only one!"

Maddy paused a second before she moved on to another thick head of hair. "Don't worry, Poppy," she said, touching her arm. "I'll get to your hair right away!" She looked at all the full chairs. "Well, as soon as a station opens up, anyway."

"No problem," Poppy reassured the busy hairdresser. "I'll just say hello to ... *Branch?!*"

Poppy was surprised to see her friend Branch sitting in a chair with curlers in his blue hair. He shifted in his seat uncomfortably. "Hi, Poppy," he muttered.

She walked over to him. "So you're going to the big party?"

"Yup," Branch said.

"But I thought you didn't like big loud parties," Poppy said.

"That was before we became friends with the Bergens," he explained. "Now I guess parties are pretty safe. As long as they're not too loud," he groused.

Poppy reached out to touch one of the curlers in Branch's hair. "And you're having your hair done for the party."

Branch drew back from Poppy's hand, a little embarrassed. "Nothing wrong with looking your best, is there?" Secretly, Branch wanted to look good for Poppy.

"Nothing at all!" Poppy agreed, nodding her head. She wanted to look good for Branch, too. "I think it's great that you're getting your hair done. It's just that I don't think I've ever seen you in here before."

"Well, this is my first time," Branch admitted. He leaned forward and whispered, "Am I doing everything right?"

"You're doing everything perfectly!" Poppy said, laughing. "You're sitting still, and you're not squirming. When Maddy works on your hair, do you chat with her?"

Branch looked puzzled. "About what?"

"Oh, anything," Poppy said. "The weather, her family, the big party tonight, scrapbooking…"

Branch shrugged. "Not really. She's so busy, she just runs up, does something to my hair, and runs off again."

Branch was certainly right about Maddy being super-busy. Her own swirl of blue hair kept moving around the salon constantly. She used a Trimmerbug to snip the ends of Guy Diamond's long, silvery hair. To reach the top tips, she had to climb on to a step-toadstool.

"Remember to sprinkle on plenty of glitter," Guy said in his shimmery voice. It sounded as though he were speaking through a microphone with reverb and electronic effects added to his voice. But that was just the way Guy talked all the time.

"Don't worry," Maddy reassured him. "I will!"

"And if you run out of glitter..." Guy Diamond shook off a cloud of silver glitter, "...there's plenty more where that came from!"

But Maddy was already moving on to her next client. She grabbed a Blowbug and aimed it at Satin and Chenille's pink-and-blue hair. *WHOOOOSH*! The Blowbug blew hot air on to their damp hair, right at the spot where the twins' hair joined them together.

"Is our hair almost dry?" Satin asked.

"Almost!" Maddy answered, working the Blowbug back and forth.

"Good!" Chenille said. "We need to get back to our dress shop soon!"

"We've got to have plenty of time to finish our outfits for tonight!" Satin explained.

"You will!" Maddy promised. "Don't worry!"

Maddy set the Blowbug in a little basket and picked up a Brusherfly. As she held it over DJ Suki's head, the Brusherfly pulled its long legs through her orange hair, brushing it. "I think you're going to have to take off your headphones," Maddy told DJ Suki.

"WHAT?" DJ Suki said loudly. "I CAN'T HEAR YOU WITH MY HEADPHONES ON."

Maddy gently lifted one of the headphones. "Please take these off so I can get to the hair around your ears."

DJ Suki laughed. "Oh, yeah! That makes total sense!" She took off her headphones and set them down. "How about some tunes? I brought my Wooferbug!"

7

Next to DJ Suki was her funky Wooferbug. She scratched its back, and it started pumping out a thumpin' dance tune! DJ Suki snapped her fingers. "That's more like it! Yeah! This is my jam! Feel the beat!"

Maddy smiled and nodded. The beat of the music inspired her to move around her salon even faster. She'd have all these Trolls ready for the big party in no time!

The first customer to be finished was Cooper. Since he wore a hat all the time, styling his hair was simple. Maddy just had to clean and trim his blue dreadlocks, add a little acorn oil, and ... *voila*! The giraffe-like Troll was ready for that night's celebration!

"Thanks, Maddy!" Cooper said, admiring his reflection in a mirror. "Terrific job, as always! You're the best!"

"Thanks, Cooper!" Maddy said. "What are you going to wear to the party?"

Cooper scrunched up his face, concentrating. "I'm still not sure. But I'm leaning towards my green hat."

Maddy smiled and nodded. That made sense, since Cooper always wore his green hat.

"Here, Poppy," Cooper said, patting the seat of the chair he'd been sitting in. "You can take my seat. I'm all done!"

"Thanks, Cooper!" Poppy said, settling on to the poofy cushion. "You look great!"

"Aw, thanks," Cooper said, looking shy. He may even have blushed a little, but since his face was already pink, it was hard to tell. There was an extra spring in his step as he practically danced out the door.

"I'll get started on you in just a second, Poppy,"

Maddy promised. She rushed over to Fuzzbert, who was sitting in a chair waiting patiently. "So," Maddy asked. "What are we doing today? Trim? New hairdo? Full cut? Perm?"

"UNG GUNG HRM GRN!" Fuzzbert grunted in his own special language, his voice muffled by the long green hair that covered his mouth. In fact, Fuzzbert was completely covered in hair, except for his feet and toes.

"OK," Maddy said a little uncertainly. "How about we start with a wash?"

Making happy little sounds, Fuzzbert nodded with his whole hairy body. Maddy asked him to lean back into the sink, and got to work shampooing his long hair. It took a lot of shampoo, but luckily Maddy had bottles and bottles of shampoo and conditioner in her cupboard. When you worked on Trolls' hair, you went through a lot of shampoo.

Sitting and waiting her turn, Poppy reached down into the basket next to her chair and pulled out the latest issue of *Troll Life*. Just as she started reading an article titled, "Cupcakes – Can You Really Ever Have Too Many?" the front door of the Hair in the Air Salon banged open.

A deep voice shouted, "HELP!"

CHAPTER 2

The deep loud voice belonged to Smidge, one of the smallest Trolls around. Though her body was little, her voice was big. And she was strong, too, able to lift heavy weights with her long blue hair. But right now, she looked scared.

Poppy rushed over to her short friend. "What's the matter, Smidge?"

"It's Karma!" Smidge said in an even deeper voice than usual. "She's missing!"

"Missing?" Poppy asked. "What do you mean? Since when?"

Everyone in the salon had gone quiet, listening to Smidge. DJ Suki tapped her Wooferbug, signalling the critter to stop playing music. You could hear a pin drop. In fact, Guy Diamond dropped a hairpin, and everyone turned to say, "Shhh!"

"Sorry," Guy whispered, carefully picking up the pin and holding on to it tightly with both hands.

"I went out into the woods with Karma," Smidge explained. "She wanted to pick an extra-special flower to put in her hair for the big party tonight."

Everyone nodded. That made sense. They knew Karma loved to weave all kinds of natural things into her hair – flowers, leaves, shells ... even sticks. Once Poppy had seen Karma try to balance a boulder in her hair, but it kept falling out.

"She led the way since she knows all the secret paths through the forest," Smidge continued. "After a while we found a field full of flowers different from any we'd ever seen before. They were so beautiful! And they smelled wonderful ... almost as good as a fresh batch of spiced cupcakes!"

Several of the Trolls licked their lips. They could go for a warm cupcake right now! But then they'd miss the rest of Smidge's tale...

"Karma decided to pick one of the strange flowers for her hair. But she wanted to pick just the right one, the one that would look the best. She wandered deep into the field of flowers. They grew so tall that I lost sight of her!" Smidge looked upset.

"That's all right, Smidge," Poppy said reassuringly. "Go on. Tell us what happened to Karma."

"I really don't know what happened to her!" Smidge cried. "All I know is, I heard this loud buzzing sound. It came, and then it went away. And when I looked for Karma, I couldn't find her anywhere! I shouted her name as loudly as I could, but she didn't answer!"

The Trolls looked concerned. When Smidge shouted, you answered. She was a very good shouter.

"Finally," Smidge said, "I ran back here to the village calling for help!"

Poppy took Smidge's tiny hand. "You did the right thing, Smidge. We've got to go back and find Karma. She may be in trouble!"

"But your hair isn't done yet!" Maddy protested. "In fact, I haven't even started on yours, Poppy. And I know you want it to be perfect for the party tonight."

"That's true, but some things are even more important than hair," Poppy said.

"Really?" Guy Diamond asked, amazed. "Are you sure about that?"

"Poppy's right," Maddy said, nodding. "I'll close

the salon, and we'll go find Karma."

Poppy thought about this. "I don't think we all need to go. Just a small group. That way we'll travel faster, and it'll be easier to stick together."

With curlers still in his hair, Branch stood up. "I'll go," he said firmly.

"No," Poppy said, gently pushing him back down into his chair. "You stay. It's your very first time in Maddy's salon! Maddy, you stay open and keep working on everyone's hair. It's what you do best! I'll go back into the forest with Smidge. DJ Suki, will you come with us? And you two, too, Satin and Chenille?"

"Us two, too!" the twins agreed.

"Let's go!" DJ Suki cried. "I'm ready to drop the beat on this search!"

Poppy turned to her small friend. "Lead the way, Smidge!"

At first, the five Trolls made good time through the woods. They were worried about their friend Karma, and it was a fine, sunny morning, so they hurried along with nothing to slow them down. Tunebugs and Critterchords sang happy melodies in the sunshine.

But then the Trolls came to a fork in the path. Smidge, leading the way, stopped and stared at the two paths in front of her.

"What's wrong, Smidge?" Poppy asked when she saw the little Troll just standing there.

"I'm not sure which way to go," Smidge admitted. "When we came here before, I just followed Karma. You know how good she is at finding her way through the forest. She loves to go exploring."

"I know," Poppy said. "Nobody loves nature more than Karma."

"Well, do you have a *feeling*..." Satin said.

"...about which path might be the right one?" Chenille asked, finishing her twin's question.

Smidge thought hard. Then she pointed to the path on the left. "I think the field of flowers might be this way, but I'm really not sure."

"That's OK," Poppy said. "Let's try it! And if at some point you realize we're going the wrong direction, we'll just turn around, come back, and try the other path. OK? Come on!"

Poppy strode confidently down the left path. Smidge, Satin, Chenille and DJ Suki followed her, making their way deeper and deeper into the forest.

Soon they found themselves in a part of the woods that was full of twigs. There were twigs on the ground. Twigs covering the path. Twigs sticking off branches. Twigs falling down from the trees. It almost seemed as though it were raining twigs!

"There sure are a lot of twigs in this forest," Satin said.

DJ Suki jumped over a pile of twigs in the path. "Don't all forests have twigs?"

"Sure," Chenille agreed. "But this has got to be the twiggiest forest I've ever seen!"

In no time at all, the Trolls' hair was full of twigs. As fast as they reached up to pluck twigs out of their hair, more twigs fell down, getting tangled up.

"I've heard of sticky hair, but this is ridiculous," Poppy said, trying to make a joke.

Suddenly Smidge yelped, "Something just flew in my hair!"

"Let me guess," Satin said. "A twig?"

"No!" Smidge insisted. "Something ALIVE!"

Poppy ran over and parted Smidge's long, thick blue hair. Deep inside, she could see an odd little striped bird with a long beak and a short tail. "I see it!" she cried. "It looks like some kind of bird! But I've never seen one like it before."

"What's it doing in my hair?!" Smidge cried. "Building a nest?"

Just then, the tiny bird flew out of Smidge's hair with a twig in its mouth. "It may be building a nest," Poppy said, "but not in your hair. It pulled out a twig!"

"That's good, I guess," Smidge said. "I wish it'd pull them ALL out!"

DJ Suki squeaked. One of the little birds had flown into her hair, too! Another swept into Poppy's hair! When they emerged, they had twigs in their mouths.

"It's OK," Poppy said, trying to calm down the

other Trolls. "They just want to clean the twigs out of our hair. We should thank them!"

"I would," Chenille said, "but I don't speak Bird."

"I don't think this is the way Karma and I came," Smidge said, pulling another twig out of her hair. "Maybe we should go back and try the other path."

Before Poppy could answer, a dark shadow passed over the trail. A much bigger bird swooped down and grabbed a twig stuck in Satin and Chenille's hair. The big bird tried to yank the twig free, but the stick was tangled up in the Trolls' thick hair. The bird flew off, carrying the twins high up into the air!

"POPPY!" they screamed as they rose into the sky. "SAVE US!"

CHAPTER 3

"**W**E'RE COMING!" Poppy shouted, racing off in the direction she'd seen the big bird fly with the twins. Smidge and DJ Suki ran after her, leaping over piles of twigs, trying to keep up as best as they could.

The twins' cries for help grew fainter and fainter.

Poppy kept looking up, trying to spot the bird. More than once, she tripped over a twig and fell. But she got right back up and kept on running.

Breathing hard, Poppy stopped for a moment and stared up at the tops of the tall trees. Where was the bird? And where were Satin and Chenille? Had the bird dropped them?

"There!" Smidge cried, pointing up with her long blue hair. Poppy and DJ Suki looked where the sharp-eyed little Troll was pointing. They spotted the bird heading for the top of the tallest tree in the woods. They could just make out its nest, perched at the very pinnacle of the tree. The big bird landed in its nest and folded its wings.

"What's that bird doing with Satin and Chenille?" DJ Suki asked.

"I think she wanted the twig in their hair, not them," Poppy said. "It's hard to tell from down here, but I bet her nest is built of twigs."

"I just hope she isn't planning to feed Satin and Chenille to her young," Smidge said. DJ Suki and Poppy stared at her with their mouths hanging open. What an awful thought!

"Come on!" Poppy cried. "We've got to climb that tree!"

The three Trolls ran as fast as they could to the base of the towering tree. They stood there, craning their necks, looking up to the top.

It was an awfully long way.

DJ Suki jumped up and wrapped her arms around the tree's trunk. She slowly slid right back down to the ground. "This isn't going to be easy," she said gloomily as she plucked a splinter out of her butt.

Poppy pointed at the tree's lowest branch. "Smidge! You can use your hair to lift me up to that branch!"

"If *you* believe it, *I* believe it!" Smidge said.

Poppy jumped on top of Smidge's hair. Using all her strength, the little Troll lifted her friend up to the branch. "You did it!" Poppy shouted down. "Now it's DJ Suki's turn!"

Smidge quickly lifted DJ Suki up to the branch. Then Poppy and DJ Suki hauled Smidge up by her own hair. Once they were all on the branch, they could see that the branches above them were closer together. Whipping their hair up, they were able to lasso the higher branches and swing themselves up.

As they reached the higher branches of the tree, the wind picked up, and the trunk swayed back and forth. "Hold on tight!" Poppy warned. "Wrap your hair all the way around each branch before you swing yourself up!"

"*I'm swinging up, so you'd better get this rescue started!*" DJ Suki sang as she made her way up the tree. The others laughed.

After climbing a few more branches, they saw it – the nest!

But were Satin and Chenille inside? Or had they been fed to hungry young birds?

"Satin!" Poppy hissed, not wanting to get the big bird's attention. "Chenille! Are you in there?"

"YES!" the twins hissed back. "GET US OUT OF HERE!"

Poppy, Smidge and DJ Suki carefully sneaked up to the bottom of the big nest. Poppy had been right – it was made out of twigs, just like the one the bird had tried to pluck from Satin and Chenille's hair. "If we pull out some of these bottom twigs," Poppy whispered, "maybe we can make an escape hole for the twins."

They started yanking out twigs, dropping them to the forest floor far below. Soon they'd opened up a hole big enough for a Troll to crawl through. (As long as the Troll wasn't Biggie.) "Satin! Chenille!" Poppy whispered. "This way! Come on out!"

SQUAWK! Instead of the twins, the big bird stuck its long, sharp beak through the hole!

Without thinking, Smidge screamed at the bird in her deep, loud voice! "GO! GO! GET OUT HERE! YOU GO AWAY! NOW!"

At the same time, DJ Suki used two twigs in her hands to beat on the trunk of the tree. She automatically drummed out a dance beat. *THWACK THWACK THWACK-ATA THWACKA THWACKA THWACK!*

Startled by the Trolls' screaming and drumming, the bird lifted off her nest and flew away! Satin and Chenille scrambled down through the hole and out of the nest, dropping on to the branch their friends were standing on.

"Thank you!" Satin exclaimed, hugging Poppy.

"We knew you wouldn't let us down!" Chenille added.

"No, but now we have to get down from this tree before that bird comes back," Poppy said, "and it's a long way!"

Swooping their hair around the next lower branch and then swinging down to land on the one below it, the Trolls made quick progress down the tree.

When they reached the lowest branch, Poppy jumped off, formed her hair into a staircase, and walked down to the ground. Soon all five of them were safely back down on the floor of the forest.

The only problem was, they were lost.

"How will we ever find Karma?" Smidge moaned, shaking her head.

"We'll find her!" Poppy promised. "Don't worry! Come on, let's go this way!" She walked confidently towards what seemed to her to be the lightest, brightest, friendliest part of the forest.

Gradually, as they marched along, the trees in the forest started to give way to huge mushrooms that towered over the Trolls. Even though the mushrooms were gigantic, they were comforting. Trolls loved mushrooms. They used them as chairs, sofas, umbrellas, tents – even dance floors, in a pinch.

"Good ol' mushrooms," DJ Suki said, giving the trunk of a purple mushroom with sparkly gold stripes a friendly pat.

SCREEEECH!

The Trolls covered their ears. What was that?!

The enormous mushroom reared back and gave another screech. *SCREEEECH!* Its cry was echoed by the other mushrooms, and the air was filled with the loud, deafening screeches of the mushrooms!

"WHAT KIND OF MUSHROOMS ARE THESE?" Satin shouted into Poppy's ear.

"I THINK THEY'RE SCREECHING MUSHROOMS!" Poppy yelled back.

"I'VE NEVER HEARD OF SCREECHING MUSHROOMS!" Chenille bellowed.

"I NEVER WANT TO HEAR OF THEM AGAIN!" DJ Suki screamed.

Covering an ear with one hand and beckoning with the other, Poppy urged the others to follow her out of the Forest of Screeching Mushrooms. "FOLLOW ME!" she shouted. "WE'VE GOT TO GET OUT OF HERE BEFORE WE GO DEAF!"

As they ran past the thick stems of the giant mushrooms, the screeching seemed to get louder and louder. *SCREEECH! SCREEEECH! SCREEEEEEEEEEECH!!!*

Finally, they left the last screeching mushrooms behind. Exhausted, they collapsed on to soft, mossy mounds of dirt. Gasping, they lay on the ground, cautiously taking their hands off their ears. In the distance, they could hear the mushrooms' screeching dying down.

"Smidge, do you remember these screeching mushrooms?" Poppy asked.

"Nope," Smidge said. "I think maybe I picked the wrong path!"

"What were those mushrooms so upset about?" DJ Suki wondered.

"I guess they just REALLY..." Satin began.

"...don't like being patted!" Chenille finished.

The Trolls sat up and looked around. Now they weren't just lost – they were really, truly, hopelessly lost.

"Which way should we go?" Satin asked.

"Well..." Poppy said, trying to decide which direction looked best.

"May I help you?" a voice asked.

CHAPTER 4

"**W**ho said that?" Poppy asked, looking around. All she saw was a small clump of dirt.

But then the clump of dirt moved towards them, and the Trolls realized it had a face, two arms and two legs. "Hi," the clump of dirt said in a friendly voice as it waved hello. "I'm Clay."

"OK," Satin said, "but what's your name?"

Clay winced. "Ooo, I am so tired of that joke. Ever since the first day of Dirt School. Thanks so much, Mum and Dad, for naming me Clay."

"Sorry," Satin said. "I was just a little confused.

So your *name* is Clay."

"Yes," Clay said, nodding his clumpy head.

Poppy walked right up to the strange little fellow, offering him her hand to shake. "Nice to meet you, Clay! I'm Poppy, and this is Satin, Chenille and Smidge."

Clay shook her hand. "Nice to meet you, too! We don't see a lot of Trolls around this part of the forest." He leaned in and peered at their heads. "Especially with so many twigs in their hair."

"Speaking of Trolls," Poppy said, plucking out a long twig and tossing it aside, "have you happened to see another Troll today? She has long green hair…"

"With sticks and flowers in it," Smidge added. "On purpose."

"And she's wearing a two-piece outfit," Satin said.

"Pale yellow, with a scalloped skirt," Chenille said.

"Really cute material, and a nice design," Satin explained.

"Really cute," Chenille agreed. "We made it. You see, we've loved fashion since we were just little Trolls, so we decided to become clothing designers, and—"

"Have you seen her?" Poppy interrupted. "Her name's Karma, and she's missing."

Clay shook his head. "Nope. You're the first Trolls I've seen in ages. I'm sorry. I wish I knew where your missing friend is. Where did you last see her?"

Smidge stepped forward. "It was in a field of tall, beautiful flowers. They smelled like spiced cupcakes warm out of the oven."

"Do you have any idea where a field like that

might be?" Poppy asked.

The little guy made out of dirt thought hard. Then he slowly started to nod. "Yes," he said. "Yes! I think I might know the field you're talking about. Right now it's full of blooms. Beautiful flowers. Nice smell. Pretty colours."

Poppy was excited. Clay seemed to know about the field they were searching for! "Could you please tell us the quickest way to get there?" she asked. "We're awfully worried about our friend."

Turning around, Clay pointed towards a stream. "Do you see that stream over there? The fastest way to get to the flower field is to float down that stream. It'll take you right to the field."

"That's great!" Poppy cheered. "Do you think you might be able to come with us and show us the way?"

All of a sudden Clay looked very nervous. He shook his head rapidly from side to side. "N-n-no!" he stammered. "I couldn't do that! No way!"

"Why not?" DJ Suki asked curiously.

"Because," he explained, looking a little embarrassed, "I never travel on water. If I fell out of the water, I'd become ... muddy. And I do NOT like to be muddy! I just ... go all to pieces."

Clay was clearly upset thinking about falling into a stream of water. Poppy softly touched his arm to reassure him. "That's OK," she said. "You don't have to come with us. We've very grateful for the information you've given us! You've been terrific!"

"I have?" Clay said, brightening. He stood up straight. "Thank you! Come with me, and I'll show you where there are some good leaves for building boats! I mean, I assume they're good for building boats. I've never built one myself." He paused.

"Boats." He shuddered.

"Thank you!" Poppy said. "Lead on!"

Clay led the way towards the stream of clear water, keeping a safe distance so he couldn't possibly slip and fall in. Before they reached the brook, he showed the Trolls a plant with big, shiny green leaves. "These leaves are perfect for making boats, I'm told. They're strong, but they float and keep out water."

DJ Suki climbed up the plant, shinned out to the end of a stem, and put her full weight on it until a leaf in front of her touched the ground. Smidge used her great strength to pluck the leaf off the stem. SPROING! The stem sprang back and forth, with DJ Suki holding on for dear life! "WHOOOAAAH!" she yelled as the plant whipped back and forth.

Working together, the Trolls picked enough leaves to make two boats. "But how will we put the leaves together?" Poppy wondered.

"I know!" Satin said. "We'll SEW them together!"

"Great idea!" Chenille said. "I always carry a couple of needles with me, just in case." She pulled out her handy portable sewing kit. "But what'll we use for thread?"

The Trolls were stumped for a second. Then Clay shyly suggested, "Your hair?" Since he hadn't had much experience with Trolls, he wasn't sure if this suggestion would offend them. But their hair looked strong – perfect for lashing leaves together to make a couple of small boats.

"Perfect!" Poppy said. "Smidge, is it all right if we use your hair? It's the longest and strongest."

"Be my guest," Smidge said in her deep voice. She plucked several long blue hairs from her head and handed them to Satin and Chenille. They threaded the hairs through the eyes of their needles and swiftly sewed the shiny green leaves together until they had two small boats, perfect for five Trolls to float in!

As they carried their boats to the creek, Clay said, "When the stream splits in two, make sure you go to the right. That way will take you straight to the flower field. The other way won't!"

"Got it!" Poppy said. "Go to the right!"

"How are we going to steer our boats?" DJ Suki asked.

"Good question," Poppy said. "I think we need to make oars."

All five Trolls looked around for something to make oars out of. Smidge spotted a tree with just the right kind of bark – curved and strong, but not so strong that they couldn't snap it into the size they wanted. They broke off some bark and cracked it into pieces that were just the right size for a Troll to paddle with.

With Clay at a safe distance, they found a good spot along the stream to put their boats in the water. Poppy and the twins climbed into one boat, while DJ Suki and Smidge got in the other. They pushed off from the bank and were swept downstream by the flowing water. As they steered with their oars, they called back to Clay, "Thank you! Thank you so much for all your help!"

"You're welcome!" he called, cupping his dirty hands around his dirty mouth. "And remember, KEEP TO THE RIGHT!"

The water was moving fast, so the Trolls made great time. "Woo hoo!" Poppy whooped. "This sure beats walking!"

As they skimmed along in their green leaf boats, the Trolls enjoyed the rush of the air blowing their hair back and the spray of water from the bows.

"Sweet!" DJ Suki shouted.

But then they noticed that the water was flowing even faster. And faster, and faster...

CHAPTER 5

WHOOSH! The Trolls' little boats were zooming along through whitewater rapids! They bounced up and down, with water splashing into their boats. Using their paddles, they worked hard to keep from capsizing!

"Now I know why Clay never went in this stream!" Satin shouted over the roar of the rapids.

"He never went in ANY stream!" Chenille yelled. "He had no idea what this would be like!"

"Try to steer for the calmest part of the water!" Poppy called out to her boatmates.

"WHAT calm part?" Chenille asked. "It all looks wild to me!"

As they struggled to keep their boats upright in the churning water of the stream, DJ Suki and Smidge were swept ahead of Poppy, Satin and Chenille. With only two Trolls in it (one of them very small), DJ Suki and Smidge's boat was much lighter than Poppy, Satin and Chenille's.

"Stay together!" Poppy called to Smidge and DJ Suki. "We've got to stay together!"

"How?" Satin asked. "We forgot to give our boats brakes!"

Poppy and the twins watched helplessly as DJ Suki and Smidge's boat swiftly approached the split Clay had told them about. To their dismay, they saw the front boat being swept to the left! It passed the split, zooming down the left channel!

"But that dirt guy said to go to the right!"

Chenille shouted.

"I don't think they had any choice," Poppy said. "The current was too strong. They just got carried off to the left. Which means we've gotta go to the left, too! We can't abandon our friends!"

All three Trolls pushed their oars into the water, steering their boat to the left. But it wasn't really necessary. The water was pulling them straight towards the left channel of the stream anyway. When they reached the split, they were nowhere near going into the right channel.

"So much for our quick and easy path to the flower field!" Satin said. "Maybe we should have asked the dirt guy what this way leads to!"

Poppy craned to see around the spray of white water coming off their bow. "Can you see Smidge and DJ Suki's boat?" she asked the twins.

"There!" Chenille cried, pointing ahead. "I

saw them for just a second before the stream bent. They're not too far ahead of us!"

"Then let's try to catch up with them," Poppy said. "Paddle!"

The three Trolls paddled as hard as they could. Even though the water was still moving fast, their paddling made a difference. They sped up. And before too long, they saw DJ Suki and Smidge's boat ahead of them. "There they are!" Poppy shouted. "We're catching up!"

"WATCH OUT FOR THAT BOULDER!" Satin and Chenille screamed.

Poppy had been so intent on spotting Smidge and DJ Suki that she didn't notice a big rock rising up out of the water right in front of them. All three Trolls dived for the left side of the boat, leaning as far as they could without tipping the boat over. The boat swerved to the left, barely missing the rock. The leaves scraped against its rough surface, but they didn't tear, and the stitches made with Smidge's hair held – for the moment.

"Whew!" Poppy gasped. "That was WAY too close!"

In the front boat, Smidge and DJ Suki had been glancing back whenever they could take their eyes off the rough water in front of them, searching for the other boat. They'd been worried that Poppy and the twins hadn't followed them when they were swept into the left channel of the raging creek.

"There they are!" Smidge bellowed. "They almost hit that same rock we almost hit!"

"POPPY! SATIN! CHENILLE!" DJ Suki yelled. "CATCH UP WITH US! WE'LL TRY TO SLOW DOWN!"

Even though the boats didn't have brakes, the Trolls did have oars, which they used to paddle against the force of the stream, straining to slow themselves down. Finally, Poppy's boat caught up, and the two boats were side by side again.

"I'm so glad to see you!" Poppy cried.

"Sorry we went the wrong way," DJ Suki apologized. "We couldn't help it. The current was way too strong."

"I know," Poppy said. "It was too strong for us, too. But the important thing is, we're back together, so there's nothing to worry about."

"Actually, there is," Satin and Chenille said, pointing up ahead.

Further downstream, they saw the falling water and rising mist that could only mean one thing...

...a waterfall!

CHAPTER 6

"A waterfall!" Satin shouted.

"WE'RE ALL GONNA DIE!" Chenille screamed.

"Oh no we're not!" Poppy said confidently. "PADDLE! PADDLE AS HARD AS YOU CAN! WE'VE GOT TO GET TO THE SHORE BEFORE WE REACH THAT WATERFALL!"

The five Trolls started paddling like mad, steering their two boats towards the left shore. The water was still moving rapidly, sweeping towards the waterfall ahead. They could hear the roar of the falls, and saw thick mist rising from the churning rapids far below.

In fact, it was so misty that their hair was soaked. It drooped down over their faces. They had to keep pushing their hair out of their eyes so they could see where they were going.

"Lean left!" Poppy said. "That'll help steer the boats to the left bank of the creek!"

DJ Suki leaned so far to the left, she almost fell into the water! Smidge whipped her wet hair around DJ Suki's waist and yanked her back into the boat. Lucky for DJ Suki, Smidge was strong enough to pull her in!

"Thanks!" DJ Suki gasped.

"Don't mention it!" Smidge bellowed politely.

Poppy, Satin and Chenille paddled their leaf boat as hard as they could. They were getting closer to the shore, but they were also still moving downstream towards the roaring falls. Poppy spotted a tree leaning over the water and got an idea.

"Smidge!" she shouted. "Try to grab that branch with your hair and pull yourself in! You've got the longest hair, and you're the strongest! If any Troll can do it, you can!"

"If *you* believe, *I* believe!" Smidge yelled back. She swung her wet blue hair around in the air over her head three times, spraying them all with water. Then she whipped her hair towards the branch. WHAP! It hit the branch, wrapping around it!

Smidge grabbed her own hair and started pulling, hand over hand, hauling her and DJ Suki's boat towards the shore. "Grab on to our boat!" she yelled to the three Trolls in the other leaf boat.

To free their hands, Poppy, Satin and Chenille dropped their oars into the water. Bobbing and sinking, the pieces of bark shot down the creek and over the falls, out of sight. The three Trolls stretched their arms towards the other boat, grabbing on to the stern. Poppy was practically pulled out of their boat. Only her toes were hooked over the edge!

"Should we climb into their boat?" Satin shouted.

"It won't hold all five of us!" Poppy yelled back. "Just stay in our boat and hold on to theirs!"

"Smidge had better hurry!" Chenille shouted. "Our stitches holding the leaves together are starting to come apart!"

"I'M HURRYING!" Smidge bawled. "GRAB ON TO EACH OTHER'S FEET!"

DJ Suki grabbed Smidge's feet. Poppy grabbed DJ Suki's feet, and Satin grabbed Poppy's feet just as Chenille grabbed Satin's. It was a Troll chain.

Just as the two boats were about to be swept over the falls, Smidge gave a mighty tug on her own hair, yanking them all on to the bank of the stream.

They flopped on to the grass like fish pulled out of the water by a fisherman.

For a moment, they just lay there, breathing hard.

"Great job, Smidge," Poppy gasped. "Thank you."

"You're welcome," Smidge panted.

"Good job, everybody," DJ Suki said. "I can't believe those boats held together in those rapids."

"They wouldn't have held together much longer," Chenille said.

"You're right," Satin agreed. "Look."

She was pointing to the stream below the waterfall. The boats had fallen completely apart, and the shiny green leaves were floating on the water. The Trolls watched them spinning and slipping past rocks in the stream. A big fish came to the surface and swallowed one of the leaves whole. *GULP!*

"OK!" Poppy said, standing up and shaking the water out of her hair like a dog. "Let's go find Karma! I'll bet we can still get back in time for the party tonight!"

The other four Trolls exchanged looks. In all the excitement, they'd forgotten about the party. It seemed impossible that they'd ever be able to rescue Karma and find their way back to Troll Village in time for the party.

But as always, Poppy stayed positive. "Come on!" she said, helping the others to their feet. "All we have to do is find that field of flowers. Maybe Karma's waiting there for us! By now she's found the perfect flower for her hair! Wait'll she sees our hair!"

The Trolls looked at each other's hair, wet and full of twigs. They started to laugh.

"Let's go this way!" Poppy urged. "I've got a

good feeling about this direction!"

"I wish I could say the same thing," Chenille muttered to Satin.

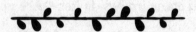

As they made their way through the woods, DJ Suki spotted something up ahead. "Look over there! Isn't that some kind of field?"

"Of flowers?" Poppy asked, excited.

"I'm not sure," DJ Suki said. "Let's run!"

But Poppy was already running, eager to see if they'd found the field of beautiful flowers Smidge had described. She dodged around trees and jumped over fallen branches, hurrying to reach the field just beyond the trees. "KARMA!" she shouted as she ran. "KARMA, WHERE ARE YOU?"

She passed the last tree and saw a field, but it wasn't full of flowers. "I don't see any blooms," she said disappointed. Only plants. Their leaves were bright red, orange and yellow, but they had no flowers or petals.

DJ Suki came up beside her. "Are you sure?" she asked. "Let's look a little closer." She stepped into the field of plants, searching for flowers, and...

SPROING! Suddenly DJ Suki was shot up into the air!

"DJ!" Poppy cried. She ran forward and...

SPROING! Poppy was sent soaring high into the sky, too!

When Satin, Chenille and Smidge ran into the field to see what was going on...

SPROING! SPROING! SPROING! All three were sprung into the air!

The plants they'd stepped on the field were Spring Plants – not plants that grow in the Spring (though they sometimes do, which is a little confusing), but plants that act like springs. When one of the Trolls stepped on one, the plant sprang up, throwing the stepper high into the air!

Unfortunately, when Poppy fell back down, she landed right on another Spring Plant! SPROING!

"AAAAAH!" Poppy yelled as she was flung into the air again.

"WWHHHHAAAAH!" DJ Suki screamed as she bounced from plant to plant.

The other three were yelling, too. "YAAAH!" "HEYYYYY!" "NOOOOO!"

Poppy tried to make a staircase out of her hair, but she was tumbling upside-down, so it was hard to aim her hair at the ground. When she finally managed to aim her hair down, it just set off another Spring Plant, sending her hair flying right back up in her face!

SPROING! SPROING! SPROING! SPROING!

If anyone had been around to witness the scene, they might have thought they were watching five Trolls bounce on dozens of trampolines, moving from one trampoline to the next, spinning and somersaulting through the air. It would have made a pretty decent act at the circus.

Finally, they were sprung past the edge of the field of Spring Plants, landing on bare ground. *THUMP! WHUMP! WHOMP! THWOMP! THUMP!* The five Trolls lay there in a heap.

"OK, so they're not flowers," DJ Suki said.

"Actually," Poppy said, "that was kind of fun! And it's a quick way to get across a field. Now let's see which way we should go. I guess I should have tried to look around while I was up in the air, but it was hard when I was tumbling upside-down." She stood up and looked around, shading her eyes with her hand.

Chenille sniffed. "Does anyone else smell a weird smell?"

The others sniffed and nodded. "Definitely," Smidge said in her bass voice.

Poppy took a step and...

CHAPTER 7

*...**S**HPLORP.*

Poppy's foot sank into the wet ground. She pulled her foot up. *SHHHPLOOP!* Grease dripped off it. "This is a marsh!" she cried. "A greasy marsh!"

"Yuck!" Satin said, lifting her foot out of the gooey ground. "This stinks. Literally."

"Well, we can't go back through that field with all the bouncy plants," Poppy said. "We've got to go on. Let's just hope this marshland ends soon."

SHPLORP.   SHPLOOP.   SHPLOP.
SHHHWURK. The Trolls walked, as best they

could, through the greasy swamp, pulling their feet out of the muck with each step. They kept their eyes peeled for stepping stones, but there weren't any.

Unfortunately, the grease wasn't just under their feet. It was dripping from above, too. The swamp trees had long, mossy branches hanging almost all the way to the ground, dripping with more grease. It dripped right into the Trolls' hair.

"Well," Poppy said, trying to look on the bright side, "maybe with all this grease in our hair, the twigs will slide out."

Satin started to giggle. "Hee hee hee!"

So did Chenille. "Heh heh heh!"

DJ Suki giggled right along with them. "Tee hee hee hee!"

And Smidge giggled the lowest, deepest giggles they'd ever heard. "Ho ho hoo hoo hoo!"

Chuckling, Poppy asked, "Why are we giggling? Did I say something really funny?"

"Hee hee, no," Satin managed to say between giggles. "Walking – hee hee hee! – through this greasy swamp – heh heh! – doesn't seem at all funny."

"Hee hee hee! But I can't help giggling!" Chenille tittered.

"It's like – hee hee! – we're being tickled!" DJ Suki chuckled.

Suddenly Poppy remembered something she'd once heard. "I think this must be the Tickle Marsh. I've heard of it, but I've never been here. Hee hee hee!"

"Ha ha, what's a Tickle Marsh?" Smidge asked.

"My dad, King Peppy, told me about it, heh heh heh," Poppy managed to say between giggles. "He found it a long time ago when he was looking for a place for us to live. Hee hee hee! The ooze in the swamp has this weird effect on anyone who gets it on them. Hee hee! It tickles them!"

Satin looked down at her feet. They were covered in ooze. "Heh heh, well, we've certainly got it on us. Hee hee! On our feet, in our hair … and even though I'm laughing, hee hee hee hee, it's not funny!"

The giggling was getting exhausting. Their stomachs were starting to hurt. The five Trolls ran, eager to escape from the Tickle Marsh. But it wasn't easy running through a swamp. *SPLAT!* DJ Suki tripped and fell face down in the mucky ooze. When she lifted her greasy face, she was still giggling. "Hee hee hee hee!"

Finally, after what seemed like ages (but was really only a few minutes), they reached the edge of the marsh, and the ground grew more solid. When they were running on dry grass, they collapsed, wiped out from all the giggling.

"I love laughing," Poppy gasped, "but that was weird."

"Agreed," DJ Suki said. "Nobody say anything funny."

Unfortunately, that struck Satin and Chenille as funny, and they started to laugh again. Smidge, Poppy and even DJ Suki herself couldn't help but join in.

"Oh, my aching stomach!" Chenille complained, still laughing.

Satin tried to run her fingers through their hair. "How are we ever going to get all this grease out of our hair?"

"Not to mention the twigs," Smidge said, pulling yet another one from her long blue hair.

Lying on the ground looking up, Poppy realized she wasn't seeing any trees above them. She glanced around, and saw they were in an open, rocky field.

There weren't any flowers, so she knew it wasn't the field Smidge had been in when Karma disappeared. But at least it looked much easier to walk through than the greasy Tickle Marsh.

As they lay there trying to recover their strength, the Trolls felt a breeze blowing. It felt good, and it smelled fresh after the stench of the marsh. But the breeze picked up, blowing harder, until it had turned from a breeze into a definite wind.

And then the wind blew harder, and harder...

CHAPTER 8

Poppy jumped to her feet. "We'd better hurry! It feels as though a big storm is coming!"

They all got up and started walking. But they hadn't taken more than a few steps when... *WHOOSH!* A gust of wind picked up Smidge, spinning her around and lifting her high into the air! It was a mini-tornado!

"WHOOOOOAAAH!" she bellowed. "HELP!"

But the four other Trolls were too busy dealing with their own mini-tornados to help Smidge. One mini-tornado twisted Satin and Chenille's hair into a terrible tangle. Another blew DJ Suki across the field. And a third picked up Poppy, flinging her up into the sky, even higher than Smidge!

Poppy looked down and saw that the field was full of mini-tornados – spinning cyclones that skimmed around the meadow, bumping into each other and flying off in opposite directions. She was spinning so fast that she was getting dizzy.

WHUMP! The mini-tornado set Poppy back down on the ground. "Try to stay together!" she shouted to the others. "We can't get separated!"

Another tiny twister picked up Satin and Chenille, spinning them up off the ground. They didn't go too high – about as high as three Trolls standing on each other's shoulders – but they spun around each other at a terrific speed. The twins managed to join hands, but their feet stuck straight out behind them as they twirled around like a pinwheel.

WHOMP! Smidge landed back on the ground. "Whew!" she groaned. "That's enough of tha—" But before she could finish her sentence, another mini-tornado whirled her up again, carrying her up even higher than before. "I DON'T LIKE THIS!" she wailed.

DJ Suki didn't get lifted high into the air, but the mini-tornados spun her all over the field, like a ballet dancer doing pirouettes. She was getting so dizzy, she was afraid she'd toss her cupcakes. "Make ... it ... stop!" she moaned. "I want to get off this ride!"

WHAM! Satin and Chenille crashed back down to the ground, still holding hands. "You OK?" Satin asked her twin.

"I think so," Chenille answered, "but our hair is a mess!"

Poppy got an idea. Maybe if the five Trolls joined hands, all of them together would be too heavy for the mini-tornados to lift off the ground. But first they had to get close enough to each other to join hands.

"Everyone get together!" Poppy shouted to the others. "We'll join hands! Maybe all together we can keep from being blown away! It'll be like Hug Time!"

Since Satin and Chenille were already holding hands, Poppy decided to try to make her way over to them. She put her head down and dug in with her feet, walking into the fierce winds, resisting being caught up in a funnel cloud.

But the strong winds kept lifting her off her feet. She thought maybe if she stayed close to the ground, she could avoid the gusts. Poppy got down on her hands and knees and crawled towards the twins.

Smidge saw that Poppy was slowly heading towards Satin and Chenille. The little Troll decided to try to use the strength of her long hair to reach them. She swung her head in a circle, whipping her blue hair around three times, then snapped it forward, aiming for Chenille's leg. On her first two tries, the wind blew her hair off course, but the third time, her hair wrapped around Satin's leg. "Close enough!" Smidge said, pulling herself slowly towards the twins.

Once Poppy and Smidge reached Satin and Chenille, they all grabbed on to each other, holding tight in the howling wind. They tried moving a few cautious steps together, and it seemed to be working – the mini-tornados weren't lifting them off the ground.

"It's working!" Satin and Chenille cried.

"Let's try to walk over to DJ Suki!" Poppy shouted.

"Where is she?" Smidge asked.

They looked around, and saw that DJ Suki was still spinning around the field, being carried from one spot to another by all the tiny twisters. Every time the clump of four Trolls tried to reach her, she went whirling off in another direction.

"DJ!" Poppy yelled. "Try to hang on to something! Anything! Then we'll come to you!"

"I'll try!" DJ Suki yelled back. "But I don't know what to hang on to! This field's pretty bare! I think everything's been blown away!"

As the mini-tornados spun her around the field, DJ Suki looked frantically for something to grab on to. There were no trees. No bushes. No rocks. Just hard-packed dirt.

But then she spotted something – a gnarled old root, sticking out of the ground.

DJ Suki got down on to the ground and crawled over to the root. She grabbed it and hung on with all her might, hoping it wouldn't come loose and pull out of the ground. Even when a twister lifted her feet off the ground, she held on to the straggly brown root.

Poppy noticed that DJ Suki had managed to grab on to something and stay in one spot. "This way!" she shouted over the roaring wind. "She's over there!"

The huddle of Trolls slowly shuffled towards DJ Suki. Their long hair whipped around their heads, sometimes slapping one of them in the face. WHAP!

When they reached DJ Suki, Poppy yelled, "Grab on to us!"

"I'm afraid to let go of this root!" DJ Suki admitted.

"It'll be OK!" Poppy said. "We'll catch you!"

Just as DJ Suki let go of the root and stretched her arm towards the cluster of Trolls, a gust picked her up and spun her around! But Smidge shot out her arm, grabbed DJ Suki's foot, and pulled her into their group hug. Poppy was so relieved, she hugged DJ Suki for real, not just to keep her close.

Now that the five Trolls were bunched together, they couldn't be lifted up and spun around by the mini-tornados. Holding on to each other tightly and shuffling along, they made their way towards the edge of the gusty field.

"Almost there…" Satin said.

"Just a few more steps…" Chenille added.

Poppy got an idea. "Wait," she said. "Even when we get out of this blowy field, we won't know which direction to go."

The others were puzzled. This didn't sound like Poppy, saying something less than positive.

"Well," DJ Suki said uncertainly, "we'll figure something out."

"Let me go," Poppy said. "I'll let one of the mini-twisters lift me up, and I'll have a good look around. From up high, maybe I'll be able to spot the flower field!"

"Or maybe you'll get blown away!" Satin said.

"We can't let you go!" Chenille agreed. "It's way too dangerous!"

"I've got an idea," Smidge said. "I'll hold on to Poppy with my hair. You all hold on to me. Then we'll let the tornado carry her up. It'll be like flying a kite!"

DJ Suki looked doubtful. "Except Poppy's not a kite. She's a Troll."

"I think it's a great idea!" Poppy said. "Let's do it!"

So Smidge wrapped the tip of her hair around Poppy's ankle. The clump shuffled a few steps back into the field of mini-tornados. Then they let go of

Poppy. She took a step or two away from the huddle ... and was twisted up into the air!

"Here I GO!!!" Poppy shouted, spinning away from them.

She quickly rose as high as Smidge's hair would let her. Smidge's hair stretched and stretched until she started to rise off the ground, but the other three Trolls held on to her feet tightly.

At first Poppy was spinning so fast that everything looked like a blur. But then she got used to the twirling and was able to focus on what she was seeing in the distance down below. Poppy spotted the edge of the field, and a forest, and a stream, and ... a field of flowers!

"I SEE IT!" Poppy yelled, but the wind was blowing so loud that the others couldn't hear her. She signalled to them, with frantic hand gestures, to pull her down.

"What's she saying?" Satin asked.

"I think she's ready to come down," DJ Suki guessed.

"OK, Smidge," Chenille said. "Reel her in! Time to land this Troll!"

With a tremendous effort, Smidge pulled her hair, and Poppy, down to the ground through the roaring, swirling wind. When she was within their reach, the Trolls reached up and pulled Poppy into their huddle.

"Did you see it?" DJ Suki asked.

"Yes!" Poppy said, breathing hard. "I saw the field of flowers! I know which way to go!"

CHAPTER
9

"**B**ut first we still have to get out of this mini-tornado field," Poppy said. "Let's head to the nearest edge, and then I'll show you which direction I think we should go."

Still in their hug formation, the five Trolls carefully shuffled across the bare ground to the edge of the field. They stepped on to grass, and the winds immediately died down. It was a relief.

"Well, we got out of that field," Satin said, "but I don't know if we'll ever get all the tangles out of our hair." They looked at each other. Each of them had a tangled mass of hair on top of their heads. The tornados had whipped their hair into crazy knots and snarls.

"At least the knots will hold in the twigs and the grease," Chenille said.

"How is *that* good?" her twin sister asked.

"Just trying to be positive," Chenille said, shrugging.

"OK, Poppy," DJ Suki said. "Which way to the flower field?"

Poppy pointed. "That way. Straight through the forest. On the other side of the woods, I saw a stream. I think it might be the one Clay told us would lead right to the field of flowers."

"All right!" Smidge said in her deep voice. "What are we waiting for? Let's get through that forest!"

They walked into the woods. There wasn't a

path, but the ground didn't have much growing out of it besides trees. The only thing they saw on the ground was nuts.

Lots of nuts.

BONK! A nut fell right on Poppy's head! Luckily, her hair was so matted and clumpy that the nut bounced right off.

"That's funny," she said to the others. "A nut just fell right on my head. What are the odds?"

BONK! BONK! BONK!

Nuts fell on Satin, Chenille and DJ Suki's heads, too!

"Ha!" Smidge laughed. "I guess I'm the only one who hasn't had a nut fall on—"

BONK! A big nut clonked Smidge right on the head. "Ow!"

The deeper they walked into the forest, the faster the nuts fell, and the bigger they got, until it seemed as if big nuts were raining down on them!

"Ouch!" DJ Suki said. "This has to be the nuttiest forest I've ever walked through!"

"Let's make it the nuttiest forest we've ever *run* through!" Satin suggested.

They started running through the storm of big nuts. But it wasn't easy, since the trees in the Forest of Falling Nuts had big, gnarled roots that curved up out of the ground. The Trolls had to leap over these roots, or duck under them. And more than once, they tripped and fell.

Lots of the big nuts got lodged in their hair, joining the twigs and the grease.

After tripping for the sixth time, Chenille was so frustrated she looked up at the trees to scream, "Stop dropping all your nuts on us!" But she only got about half of the sentence out before her mouth filled with nuts. She spat the nuts out. "PTOOEY!"

Following right behind her attached twin, Satin stepped on to the nuts and ran in place for a minute, the slippery nuts rolling under her feet. Chenille kept running, so eventually their hair jerked Satin off the pile of spat-out nuts.

Feeling a bit battered, the Trolls reached the edge of the Forest of Falling Nuts. A clear stream ran between the forest and the field of flowers.

Poppy pointed across the stream at the field. "Is that it, Smidge? Is that the field where you went with Karma so she could pick a flower for her hair?"

Smidge peered at the blooming field. Then she smiled. "Yes!" she boomed. "That's it! KARMA! ARE YOU OVER THERE?"

There was no answer.

"We've got to get across this stream and search that field," Poppy said determinedly.

They looked at the stream. The water was flowing steadily, but not as swiftly as it had been at the spot where Clay first showed it to them. It made a pleasant gurgling sound as it rippled along through stones and tree roots.

"Could we swim across?" DJ Suki said. "It doesn't look dangerous."

Poppy considered this suggestion. "I suppose we probably could, but I hate to risk anything bad happening to one of us. Remember that big fish we saw that ate the leaf from our boat?"

The other nodded solemnly. They remembered the fish with its big mouth, the perfect size for swallowing a Troll in a single bite. It wasn't pleasant to think about a fish like that lurking in the shadowy depths of this stream.

"How about a zoom rope?" Smidge suggested.

CHAPTER
10

"**A** zoom rope!" Poppy enthused. "That's a GREAT idea!"

Trolls loved to tie a rope between two trees, flip their hair over the rope, grab the end of their hair, and slide down the rope! Usually they rode zoom ropes for fun and transport around Troll Village, but they could also be a handy way to cross a stream full of hungry fish.

"What'll we use for the rope?" DJ Suki asked.

"Our hair's way too messed up with sticks and nuts and grease..." Satin said.

"...for us to plait it into a rope long enough to cross this stream," Chenille said, finishing the thought.

Poppy nodded. "That's true. But maybe we could find a vine."

"Back in that forest with all the nuts bonking us on the head?" Chenille asked, making a face.

"Let's look around," Poppy suggested. "Maybe we can find a vine without getting bonked again."

They searched the area, scanning the ground and the nearby trees without going back into the Forest of Falling Nuts.

"Found one!" Satin said, pointing at a tree near the stream. A long vine dangled down from a branch high in the tree.

"And it looks long enough!" Chenille added.

"Smidge, do you think you could pull that vine down?" Poppy asked.

"You got it," Smidge said, spitting on her hands and rubbing them together. She strode over to the vine, jumped up, and gave it a good strong yank. The vine fell at her feet, piling itself up in a neat coil.

"Chenille, Satin, you're the experts on tying knots from all your sewing," Poppy said, handing them the long vine. "Can you tie the right kind of knot in this vine for us to lasso a tree branch across the stream?"

"Totes!" Chenille exclaimed.

"No doubt!" Satin agreed. The twins went to work and tied a perfect lasso on to the end of the vine.

Since Smidge was the strongest, they picked her to toss the vine across the stream. She swung the vine around her head three times and then threw it at a branch on the other side.

She missed.

"That's OK, Smidge!" Poppy said, clapping her hands like a coach. "Just try it again! The first throw's just for measuring the distance, anyway!"

With a quick flick of her wrist, Smidge snapped the vine back to her side of the stream. Then she swung it around her head again and whipped it at the thick, broken branch.

The vine lasso looped itself around the branch!

"All right! Way to go, Smidge!" the other Trolls cheered.

Smidge pulled on the vine, and the twins' knot tightened and held. Holding the other end, she quickly climbed up a tree and tied it to a sturdy branch on their side of the stream.

The zoom rope was ready.

ZOOM! ZOOM! ZOOM! One at a time, the Trolls flipped their hair over the line, grabbed on to it, and slid across to the other side of the stream.

Poppy went last. As she zipped over the middle of the creek, a big fish leaped out of the water, snapping its jaws at her feet! "YAAAH!" Poppy screamed, lifting her feet as high as she could.

SPLASH! The big fish landed back in the brook, sending a spray of water on to the bank and soaking the other Trolls. Poppy dropped down on to the grass, shaking a little from her close call.

"REAL glad we didn't try to swim across," Chenille said.

Poppy didn't stay shaken for long. She walked towards the field full of flowers. "KARMA!" she called. "WHERE ARE YOU?" All five of them shouted Karma's name, making their way deeper into the field of beautiful flowers."

But there was no answer.

"Are you sure this is the right field of flowers, Smidge?" Poppy asked.

"Positive!" Smidge insisted. "This is it! And that's the buzzing I heard just before Karma disappeared!"

They all heard it. A loud buzzing that got louder and louder...

"Where is that coming from?" DJ Suki asked.

"There!" Chenille shouted, pointing to the sky.

It was a huge Stingerbug, bigger than three Trolls put together! Bigger than Biggie! And it was diving straight at them! *BZZZZZZ!!!*

"HIT THE DIRT!" Smidge yelled in her deep voice. All five Trolls dived for the ground, just as the Stingerbug swooped down right where they'd been standing. Just before he hit the ground, he pulled up, climbing back into the sky.

But he circled around again.

"HERE HE COMES AGAIN!" Satin warned.

The Stingerbug went into another steep dive. *BZZZZZZ!!!* He was coming right at them!

"Spread out!" Chenille hissed. "Hide!"

The Trolls separated, scrambling to hide underneath the tall blooming flowers. The Stingerbug skimmed right over the tops of the flowers, inches above the Trolls' heads. His buzz was furiously loud. *BZZZZZ!!!*

"This is ridiculous!" Poppy said, standing up. "I'm not hiding any more!"

Overhead, the gigantic flying creature was preparing to dive at the Trolls again.

"Poppy, get down!" Satin whispered. "That thing'll sting you, or bite you, or knock your head off!"

"Or maybe," she said bravely, "it'll answer my questions!"

She looked up at the diving critter, cupped her hands around her mouth, and called, "Hello! My name is Poppy! Why are you trying to drive us away? And have you seen our friend Karma?"

The huge bug pulled up abruptly and hovered right over Poppy, still buzzing angrily. "Begone!" it commanded in its buzzing voice. "Access to this place is strictly restricted! You have no right to be here!"

Poppy looked confused. "No right to be in a field full of beautiful flowers? Why?"

"Because," the Stingerbug growled, "these beautiful flowers belong to the Queen! It is FORBIDDEN to walk among them! And it is ABSOLUTELY FORBIDDEN to pick them! Anyone caught picking these flowers will be carried off to the palace!"

"That must be what happened to Karma!" Smidge whispered. "She probably picked a flower!"

This gave Poppy an idea. Staring defiantly into the Stingerbug's big dark eyes, she reached out and seized the stem of the nearest tall flower.

The Stingerbug looked alarmed. "Don't you dare!" he warned.

SNAP! Poppy plucked the flower!

The critter gasped! "You dare?!"

"Oh, yeah," Poppy said calmly. "I dare."

The other four Trolls exchanged a quick look. Following Poppy's lead, each of them grabbed a flower and pulled. SNAP! SNAP! SNAP! SNAP! All four of them picked flowers!

"THAT'S IT!" the Stingerbug roared. "YOU'RE ALL GOING TO THE PALACE!"

He gave a loud, higher-pitched buzz, and four more Stingerbugs swooped in over the field. The first Stingerbug picked up Poppy, and the new arrivals swept up Satin, Chenille, DJ Suki and Smidge.

They were all headed to the palace. Which is exactly what Poppy wanted…

CHAPTER
11

The Stingerbug Queen's palace hung high in the branches of an enormous tree. As the Stingerbugs carried the Trolls up towards it, they saw that the palace was shaped like a Troll pod, only upside-down, with the thickest part at the top and the pointy part at the bottom. But it wasn't soft and colourful. It looked as though the palace were made out of some hard, drab material, like dried mud. And it was much, much bigger than any Troll pod.

"Some palace," Chenille murmured to Satin.

"They could definitely use some help with their

design and outside décor," Satin agreed.

The Stingerbugs flew through an arched entrance near the bottom of the palace. Once inside, they flew through long, wide halls filled with buzzing bugs. "Make way!" the biggest Stingerbug growled. "Make way! We carry prisoners for the Queen! FLOWER-PICKERS!"

Angry buzzes of disapproval came from the crowds of Stingerbugs as the Trolls passed by on their way up to the Queen's Royal Chamber.

At the top of the palace, the Stingerbugs flew past guards into the Royal Chamber. The Queen was not present. The Stingerbugs put the Trolls down and ushered them into a cage with hard, beige bars. As the cage's door slammed closed behind them, the Trolls saw ... Karma!

"Karma!" they cried. "Are you all right?"

"Poppy! Smidge! DJ Suki! Satin! Chenille!"

Karma joyfully called as she ran over and hugged them. "Yes, I'm all right! But these Stingerbugs are very mad at me for picking one of their flowers."

"They're mad at us, too," Poppy said.

"Why?" Karma asked.

"Same reason," Poppy said. "But don't worry. We're going to get out of here!"

"How?" Karma asked.

Poppy hesitated. She didn't actually know how the Trolls were going to get out of the Stingerbugs' palace. She was just confident that they were going to do it. Somehow.

"ALL RISE FOR THE QUEEN!" one of the Stingerbugs ordered. The Stingerbugs in the Royal Chamber vibrated their transparent wings, rising slightly off the floor.

The Queen flew into the chamber.

She was even bigger than the Stingerbugs who

had carried the Trolls to the palace. She wore a long dark cape decorated with the petals of the flowers the Trolls had picked. At the back of her cape, the Trolls could see her long, sharp stinger.

"The Queen rules over these Stingerbugs," Karma told the other Trolls. "They do whatever she says. It's a fascinating system. I don't know whether she's elected, or inherits the throne—"

"SILENCE!" roared the Stingerbug who had announced the Queen's entrance.

The Queen took her place on a throne, next to a large column that lay on the floor. The Stingerbug who had first dive-bombed the Trolls in the flower field approached the throne.

"Your Majesty," he buzzed. "We present to you these Flower-Pickers, whom we caught in the very act of picking your flowers."

"Shameful!" the Queen said. "And criminal!

Picking my beautiful flowers is strictly against the Law of the Stingerbugs!"

Poppy stepped forward, grabbed the bars of the cage, and stuck her head through. "Your Majesty, we didn't know anything about your law. We only wanted to—"

"Ignorance is no excuse!" the Queen interrupted. "And how dare you address me directly! You, a mere commoner!"

Satin stepped forward angrily. "Poppy just happens to be OUR queen! The queen of the Trolls!"

The Stingerbugs all made a strange buzzing sound – short buzzes with spaces in between. The Trolls realized they were laughing.

"You?" the Queen sneered. "A queen? I hardly think so!"

"What are you going to do to us?" Poppy asked defiantly.

"Hm," the Queen said, appearing to be thinking it over. "I'm not sure. Perhaps we shall eat you!"

Now it was Karma's turn to laugh. "Eat us?! She's bluffing. Stingerbugs only eat nectar and honey. They'd never eat us!"

The Queen looked angry. "Perhaps not. But we could sting you. Tell me Stingerbugs don't sting!"

Poppy turned to Karma. "Do they?" she whispered. "Sting?"

"Oh, yes," Karma whispered back, nodding. "But I'll tell you another thing about Stingerbugs. They can't resist a challenge. They never turn one down! Never!"

"Interesting," Poppy whispered.

"What are you Flower-Pickers whispering about?" the Queen demanded.

"Oh, nothing, your Majesty," Poppy said. "It's just that this is the time of day when we Trolls usually challenge whoever we're with to a contest. You wouldn't be interested."

All the Stingerbugs looked intrigued. "What sort of a contest?" the Queen asked.

Poppy thought fast. "Let's see ... what day is it? Oh, yes, well, on this day of the week, we always challenge someone to a contest of ... strength. But you wouldn't be interested. On with our punishment!"

"Just a moment," the Queen said. "I will decide when it's time for punishment! First, let's have a contest of strength! Buzzer, step forward!"

From the shadows at the back of the chamber, a huge Stingerbug came forward. He was bigger than any of the other Stingerbugs, even the Queen.

The Queen smiled. "Buzzer shall serve as our champion. Who will compete for the Flower-Pickers?"

"Oh, we don't care," Poppy said casually. "We'll let you pick. But when we win, will you let us go?"

"Certainly," the Queen said, certain of victory. "But you won't win. Because I choose … THAT ONE!"

Just as Poppy had anticipated, the Queen pointed at Smidge.

All the Stingerbugs laughed their strange, buzzing laughs again.

"An excellent choice, your Majesty!" said the big Stingerbug who had captured Poppy. "We are sure to win!"

"Thank you," the Queen said. "And now, Buzzer, show these criminals what true strength looks like!"

Grinning, the huge Stingerbug walked up to the massive throne. "If you'll pardon me, your Majesty," he said in a deep buzz, gesturing for her to move off the throne.

The Queen stepped down from the throne, moving over to the fallen column that lay on the floor. Buzzer lifted the heavy seat over his head, grunting loudly. All the Stingerbugs cheered! Buzzer dropped the throne to the floor. WHAM!

"Your turn," the Queen said, sitting back on her throne. "What would you like to lift? An acorn, perhaps? We could probably find a nice little one."

The Stingerbugs laughed. "I think I'll try that throne," Smidge said. The Stingerbugs laughed even harder.

"Excellent! This should be good!" the Queen said. "Let her out of the cage!"

As the guards opened the door to the cage, the Queen started to get off her throne again. "Oh, that's all right," Smidge said. "You can stay on it."

The Stingerbugs looked confused. The Queen slowly settled back on to her throne. Smidge walked across the chamber, slipped her hair under the throne ... and lifted it high in the air with the Queen sitting on it!

The Stingerbugs all gasped! The Trolls cheered! "Yeah, Smidge! That's showin' 'em!"

Smidge gently set the throne back down. "Is this your biggest throne, Queenie?" she asked. "The way Buzzer was grunting, I thought it'd be a lot heavier."

The Queen was amazed. But she was true to her word. "You've won, and you may go." She signalled to her guards, who opened the door to the cage. The Trolls filed out.

Smidge looked at the large column that lay on the floor. "Why is this big thing lying on the floor?"

"It fell ages ago," the Queen said, "and it's too heavy to lift back into place."

"Really?" Smidge said. "Let's see!"

The tiny Troll slid her hair under one end of the

massive column and wrapped it all the way around. She braced her feet and pulled, lifting the column back into its rightful place, standing between the floor and the ceiling. She gave it a final tug, and it locked into place. CHONK!

The Stingerbugs were silent a moment, too astonished to say anything. Then they broke into loud, buzzy cheers!

The Queen jumped off her throne to stare up at the column. When she turned around, the Trolls noticed a tear in her cape.

"Um, your majesty," DJ Suki said. "You've got a rip in your royal cape."

The Queen twisted around, looking at the tear. "Yes," she sighed. "That's one of the problems with having a razor-sharp stinger. My cape's been like that for ages."

"We can take care of that!" Satin and Chenille

said. The twins whipped out their handy portable sewing kits and went to work sewing up the tear. In no time at all, the cape looked as good as new.

"Wonderful!" the Queen cried. "What a day this has been! I wish I could remember this for ever!"

"Perhaps this will help," Poppy said, stepping forward and handing the Queen a scrapbook she'd put together in the time it took the twins to fix the cape. "Luckily, I never go anywhere without my scrapbooking materials."

The Queen turned the pages, admiring Poppy's pictures of Smidge lifting the Queen, Smidge lifting the column, and the twins repairing the royal cape. "Marvellous!" she cried. "We are in your debt! If there is anything we can do for you, Queen Poppy, please let us know!"

"Well, there is one little thing," Poppy said, smiling.

CHAPTER
12

Each of the six Trolls had her own personal Stingerbug to fly her back to Troll Village. On this journey, there would be no falling twigs, or nuts, or rushing streams, or screeching mushrooms, or Spring Plants, or greasy Tickle Marshes, or mini-tornadoes. And with the swiftly flying Stingerbugs carrying them the whole way, the Trolls would make it back to their village just in time for the big party!

The Stingerbugs set them down at the edge of the village. "Thanks for the ride!" Satin and Chenille chimed.

"Yes, thank you so much," Poppy said. "We really appreciate it."

"It was our pleasure," said the Stingerbug who had dive-bombed them in the flower field. "Enjoy your party!"

He started to fly off, but then returned. "I almost forgot," he said, walking over to Karma. "The Queen asked me to give this to you." He handed her one of the beautiful flowers from the forbidden field.

"Thank you!" Karma exclaimed. "I love it!" She stuck the flower in her piled-up hair, right between a stick and a leaf. "It's perfect!"

The six Stingerbugs flew off, buzzing as they went. The Trolls waved goodbye. Then they turned and ran straight to Maddy's Hair in the Air Salon.

"Look who we found!" Poppy sang out as they rushed in through the door.

"Karma!" Maddy cried, delighted. She ran to her friend and gave her a big hug. "I was so worried. What happened? Did you get lost?"

Karma shook her head. "Not lost. Taken."

"Taken?!" Maddy asked. "By whom?"

"There'll be plenty of time to tell you the whole story later," Poppy promised. "But right now we have a party to get ready for! Can you help us with our hair?"

Maddy shook her head sadly. "Sorry, but there's no time! The party's already started. Poppy, they're expecting you to light the party torch! And DJ Suki, they need you to get the music going! You have to hurry over to the party right now! They're all waiting for you!"

"But," Satin protested, "our hair!"

Maddy pushed them out the door. "Go! Go! Go!"

The six Trolls stood outside the salon. "What are we going to do?" Chenille asked. "Our hair looks terrible!"

They looked at each other. Their hair was greasy from the marsh. It was twisted and matted from the mini-tornadoes. It had got wet from the stream and the waterfall's spray and had dried without being combed or brushed. Nuts had lodged in their hair. And it was still full of twigs – so many twigs!

"I think you look fine!" Karma said brightly. She thought you could never have too much nature in your hair.

Poppy sighed. "Well, I guess the important thing is that we're here – not what we look like. Let's just go to the party and try to have a good time. I'll light the party torch, and DJ Suki will spin some tunes, and everything'll be fine."

She said it, but she didn't really believe it. Poppy

was always positive and optimistic, seeing the bright side of things, but even she had her limits. A Troll's hair was very important to her. She always wanted it to look good. Especially at a big party!

Smidge said, "Poppy's right. The important thing is that we found Karma and rescued her from the Stingerbugs. We should go to the party and celebrate, no matter how stupid our hair looks!"

Poppy stood up straight, threw back her shoulders, and picked a twig out of her hair. "Let's do this!"

She strode off towards the party in the centre of Troll Village, followed by her five friends.

At the party, Trolls milled around. Without the party torch lit, and without music playing, it didn't really seem like a party.

Biggie looked around anxiously. "Where's Poppy?" he kept asking everyone. "And Smidge?

And Satin? And Chenille? And DJ Suki? And Karma?"

"You've already asked me that, like, a hundred times!" Branch complained. He looked splendid with the new curly hairstyle Maddy had given him. "I keep telling you, I don't know! But knowing Poppy the way I do, I'm sure she'll be here. Why are you so worried?"

"I'm not worried," Biggie lied. "But Mr Dinkles is." He stroked his pet worm's back reassuringly.

Cooper spotted the six Trolls walking towards the centre of the party. "Here they come!" he announced, pointing. Everyone turned to look at Poppy and the others.

They walked up with their wild hair. Everyone stared.

"Hi, everyone!" Poppy said a little nervously as everyone stared at her and her friends. "Come on!

Let's get this party started!"

Everyone just stood there, gawking.

"Look at their hair!" Guy Diamond finally said.

"That's ... unbelievable!" Harper sputtered.

"UNG GUH MMMNN!" Fuzzbert added.

"It's ... INCREDIBLE!" Cooper said. "I LOVE IT!"

"It's the new look!" Guy Diamond announced.

Everybody loved the way their hair looked! They all crowded around Poppy and her friends, asking how they'd got their hair to look like that!

Maddy walked up. She'd finally closed up her salon, and was ready for the big party.

"Maddy!" Guy Diamond said, running over to her. "Can you make my hair look like theirs? Please?"

"And mine?" "And mine, too?" asked lots of other Trolls, running up to Maddy.

Maddy looked puzzled. "Uh, sure," she said. "I guess. All I'll need is some grease, twigs and nuts."

Just then, Poppy lit the party torch, and DJ Suki dropped the beat on a pounding dance tune. "LET'S PARTY!" Poppy yelled, holding the burning torch high in the air. Everyone cheered!

All the Trolls partied and danced and laughed long into the night.

And the next day, Maddy's Hair in the Air Salon was crowded with customers. Carrying buckets of grease, nuts and twigs, Maddy ran from Troll to Troll, giving each of them "the new look"!

DreamWorks

Trolls

Follow Your ART

A Novel by Jen Malone

Turn the page for a sneak peek!

ONE

The Chapter with Paint Splatters and Caterbus-Fluff Moustaches

Harper

I add one final, final touch—a swoosh of teal on the king's waistcoat—to the portrait using the very tip of my hair as a paintbrush, because why not? When you have hair as incredible as a Troll's, it's kind of amazing how many uses you can find for it.

"King Peppy Looking Rad in Yarn. I think that should be your title," I tell the painting, taking a step back to admire it in its full glory. I made my depiction of our intrepid leader from braided yarn, paint, and Caterbus fluff (which captures his substantial moustache pretty impressively, I have to admit).

Not bad, Harper. Not bad at all.

A happy fizziness bubbles in my belly, just like it always does when I finish a new piece.

Time to hang this one up. I shouldn't have taken the past fifteen minutes to finish it, because I'm already running late to meet my best friend, Poppy, but I couldn't help myself. Sometimes my paintings just speak to me.

Harrrrrrrper, come play with us!

And, being a true artiste (which is exactly like an artist, but I think it sounds way cooler and more important), I have no choice but to listen.

Besides, it's part of the BFF code, to forgive and forget, so I'm pretty confident Poppy will cut me some slack if I'm running just a few minutes behind schedule. She'll understand. Everyone in Troll Village will understand, because they all get it that art is my calling. My jam. It's the thing that makes me . . . me.

I step forward again and grip the sides of the painting. I should probably give it a chance to dry completely first, but I'm running so late already and since I'm always hair-to-toe paint splatters anyway (other than my smock, which is spotless—go figure), I'm not sure it makes much difference.

Paint splatters are my signature look, I guess. Poppy likes to tell me I have the whole Roy G. Biv thing going on, with my hair being every colour of the rainbow and because I'm always covered in every shade of paint. What's a few more?

I stretch my fingertips to reach the edges of the canvas.

Twenty years ago, King Peppy led all the Trolls from the Troll Tree to Troll Village to save our lives, and I really wanted to honour his importance by making my portrait of him as lifelike as possible. So I painted him to scale, which means the picture is as tall as me.

The walls of my pod are chock-full of cheerful landscapes of Troll Village and bright collages of my friends, and of course the only empty spot would have to be all the way across the room. I hope I don't trip over any of my three-dimensional dioramas as I go . . . or the braided rug I wove from natural fibres last week.

"I could . . . sure . . . use . . . an . . . assistant!" I huff through deep breaths as I struggle under the weight of it. My hypothetical assistant would preferably have strength to spare, like my friend Smidge, so I wouldn't have to hoist paintings up to their hanging spots like this. Oof!

I glance at my potted flower on the windowsill. "What do you think? Is this my best piece yet?"

Flower doesn't talk back.

He sings!

First he unfolds his petals, then he lets loose a high-pitched "Boom-chicka-rocka!" that makes me giggle.

"Thanks," I reply.

I finally get the painting into place right next to one I did of Mr. Dinkles, a tiny pet worm my friend Biggie totally dotes on. I take a second to straighten the frame so it hangs evenly.

"Voilà!" I announce. Flower dances happily along the sill, and when his petals shimmy to the left, a spot of morning sunlight hits the floor of my pod. It must be even later than I thought.

Whoops! I've got to finish getting ready! The happy, melodic sounds of Troll Village outside my pod provide a fun energy boost for all the Trolls out there bustling about their day already. I can't wait to be part of it all.

I love everything about Troll Village. It's completely magical, all neon-bright and sinkably soft, and we're tucked away cosy and safe in a sun-splashed clearing deep in the woods. The whole place is so deliciously fuzzy it practically demands petting, from the cheerful, fluffy flowers on the fuzzy carpet of ground to our plush, multicoloured felt pods that dangle from tree branches on super-strong strands of Troll hair.

Oh, and Troll Village is always pulsing with dance music.

Yep, dance music.

Because that's how we Trolls roll.

When we're not busting a move, we're zip-lining along the tree branches or zooming down the chutes winding around the trunks or just generally whooshing from place to place.

Or hugging. Always with the hugging, because it's basically our favourite thing to do.

The sights, sounds, and textures (and hugs) of Troll Village are a non-stop explosion for the senses. But it's the colours that make the whole place really POP and make it even more perfectly perfect if you happen to be an artiste. Like me. Troll Village is full of vibrant hues any artist would go dizzy over.

And I really, really do.

The thing is, when you're so full of love for something, you mostly just want to share that feeling with everyone, and that's what today's all about. Getting me one step closer to doing exactly that.

"Today's the day, Flower," I tell him as I adjust the canvas so King Peppy is perfectly balanced, and then put my supplies away. His petals dance in reply, because today is the day when Poppy and I pick the perfect, beyond-any-Troll's-expectations, dazzle-your-hair-off opening exhibit for my new gallery.

That's right. Harper, artiste Troll, is about to become Harper, artiste Troll slash owner of Troll Village's newest business venture, a brand-new pop-up art gallery...